Amanda Pig, Schoolgirl

A Puffin Easy-to-Read

by Jean Van Leeuwen
pictures by Ann Schweninger

PUFFIN BOOKS

For Elizabeth, schoolgirl

J.V.L.

For Judy Lanfredi

A.S.

PUFFIN BOOKS
Published by the Penguin Group
Penguin Young Readers Group,
345 Hudson Street, New York, New York 10014, U.S.A.
Penguin Group (Canada), 90 Eglinton Avenue East, Suite 700, Toronto, Ontario, Canada M4P 2Y3
(a division of Pearson Penguin Canada Inc.)
Penguin Books Ltd, 80 Strand, London WC2R 0RL, England
Penguin Ireland, 25 St Stephen's Green, Dublin 2, Ireland (a division of Penguin Books Ltd)
Penguin Group (Australia), 250 Camberwell Road, Camberwell, Victoria 3124, Australia
(a division of Pearson Australia Group Pty Ltd)
Penguin Books India Pvt Ltd, 11 Community Centre, Panchsheel Park, New Delhi - 110 017, India
Penguin Group (NZ), Cnr Airborne and Rosedale Roads, Albany, Auckland 1310, New Zealand
(a division of Pearson New Zealand Ltd)
Penguin Books (South Africa) (Pty) Ltd, 24 Sturdee Avenue, Rosebank, Johannesburg 2196, South Africa

Registered Offices: Penguin Books Ltd, 80 Strand, London WC2R 0RL, England

First published in the United States of America by Dial Books for Young Readers,
a division of Penguin Books USA Inc., 1997
Published in a Puffin Easy-to-Read edition by Puffin Books,
a member of Penguin Putnam Books for Young Readers, 1999
Published by Puffin Books, a division of Penguin Young Readers Group, 2007

1 3 5 7 9 10 8 6 4 2

THE LIBRARY OF CONGRESS HAS CATALOGED THE DIAL EDITION AS FOLLOWS:
Van Leeuwen, Jean.
Amanda Pig, schoolgirl / by Jean Van Leeuwen;
Pictures by Ann Schweninger.—1st ed.
p. cm.
Summary: Amanda Pig's first day of school is every bit as wonderful as she always hoped it would be.
ISBN: 0-8037-1980-9 (hc)
[1. First day of school—Fiction. 2. Schools—Fiction. 3. Pigs—Fiction.]
I. Schweninger, Ann, ill. II. Title.
PZ7.V3273Ap 1997 [Fic]—dc20 95-53062 CIP AC

PUFFIN BOOKS ISBN 978-0-14-130357-4
Puffin® and Easy-to-Read® are registered trademarks of Penguin Group (USA) Inc.

Printed in the United States of America

Reading Level 1.9

CONTENTS

Lollipop 5

The Circle 16

The Playground 28

Pictures 38

LOLLIPOP

Finally, finally, finally

it was the day Amanda had waited for.

She hopped out of bed.

She put on her new purple party dress

and her new pink hair ribbons.

"There," said Amanda. "I'm all ready."

She went to find Mother.

"Is it time?" she asked.

Mother opened her eyes.

"Even the sun is not up yet," she said.

"You will have to wait a little longer."

"I have been waiting my whole life,"

said Amanda, "to go to school."

She played school with her animals

until the sun came up.

“Now is it time?”

she asked at breakfast.

“Not quite,” said Father.

Amanda said good-bye to Sallie Rabbit.
"Too bad you're too little for school,"
she said. "But don't worry.
I will play with you when I get home."
She tucked Sallie in for a nap.
"Now?" she asked.
"Now!" said Oliver.

At the bus stop

Mother and Father hugged Amanda.

“Have fun, schoolgirl,” said Father.

“I will!” said Amanda.

She hopped up the high bus steps

and found a seat with Oliver.

Oliver knew everyone on the bus.

"Hello, Bernard!" he called.

"Hi, Rosie. Hi, Alexander."

Soon he was talking and laughing

with his friends.

Amanda didn't know anyone. Not yet.

In the next seat was someone her size.

"Hello," said Amanda.

The someone did not answer.

She was sucking on a red lollipop.

"I like lollipops," said Amanda.

"Purple is my best flavor."

The someone did not answer.

"My name is Amanda," said Amanda.

"This is my first day of school

and I have a new dress."

The someone still did not answer.

She looked as if she were going to cry.

"Are you scared?" asked Amanda.

The someone nodded her head.

"I'm not," said Amanda. "School is fun.

You will like it. You'll see."

The bus stopped

and everyone started to get off.

"I will take you to your room,"
said Oliver.
Amanda took the someone's hand.
"Come on," she said.

Together they followed Oliver
down the high bus steps and
through the wide halls to their room.

"Good-bye," said Oliver.

"Hello," said the teacher.

"I am Mrs. Flora Pig."

"I am Amanda," said Amanda.

"And who is this?" asked the teacher.

The someone did not answer.

"This," said Amanda, "is Lollipop."

THE CIRCLE

In Mrs. Flora Pig's room
there was so much to do,
Amanda didn't know what to do first.
She played in the dress-up corner.
"Look, Lollipop," she said.
"I'm a farmer astronaut."

She played in the make-believe corner.

"I can't believe it," she said.

"A whole suitcase full of puppets.

Hi, Mr. Rabbit. You should meet

my rabbit. Her name is Sallie."

She played in the building corner.

“I never saw so many blocks,” she said.

“I’ll make a skyscraper. Or a city.

Or maybe the whole world!”

Mrs. Flora Pig’s room had giant ABC’s

and a piano and boxes called cubbies.

"Cubbies?" said Amanda.

"What are those for?"

"For things you bring to school

and the work you take home,"

said Mrs. Flora Pig.

"I want to do a lot of work,"

said Amanda.

"Soon we will," said Mrs. Flora Pig.

"But right now we are going to sit

in a circle and get to know each other."

Amanda saw a circle of little chairs
and one big one.
The big one must be for me,
she thought,
because I am so big now.
Amanda sat in the big chair.

Mrs. Flora Pig sat next to her.

But something was wrong.

Her knees were next to her ears.

"That's the teacher's chair, silly,"

said a tiny boy.

"Oops," said Amanda.

She and the teacher changed chairs.

"Now we are going to play a game,"

said Mrs. Flora Pig.

"I call it the name game."

She pointed at herself.

"My name is Mrs. Flora Pig," she said.

"And I like to play the piano."

She pointed at the tiny boy.

"My name is William," said the boy.

"And I like big trucks."

She pointed at a girl dressed in pink.

"My name is Lily," said the girl.

"And I like my baby sister."

She pointed at Lollipop.

Lollipop didn't say anything.

Instead of her lollipop,

she was sucking her thumb.

"Why doesn't she talk?" asked William.

"She will talk when she is ready,"

said Mrs. Flora Pig.

"Maybe today. Maybe tomorrow."

She pointed at Amanda.

"My name is Amanda," said Amanda. "And I like ballet and my new dress and Sallie Rabbit and ice cream and my brother Oliver and purple and singing songs.

But the very best thing I like
is being a schoolgirl."

"How nice," said Mrs. Flora Pig.

Mrs. Flora Pig played the piano

and everyone sang.

Everyone except Lollipop.

Mrs. Flora Pig read a silly story

and everyone laughed.

Everyone except Lollipop.

Then it was time to go out
to the playground.
"Oh, good!" said Amanda.
"I love swings and slides
and monkey bars."

Everyone was swinging and sliding
and climbing and jumping.
Everyone except Lollipop.

“Come on, Lollipop,” said Amanda.
“Let’s have fun.”
But Lollipop sat in the sandbox
with a sad face.

“Please don’t be sad,” said Amanda.
“I am your friend.”

"Me too," said Lily.

"Me three," said William.

"I bet I can make Lollipop smile."

He walked up the slide,

slid down very fast,

and did a somersault at the bottom.

"Ta-dah!" he said.

Amanda laughed.

But Lollipop did not smile.

"Look at me," said Lily.

She climbed high on the monkey bars,

hung upside down by her knees,

and made funny faces.

"How's that?" she asked.

But Lollipop did not smile.

“Watch this,” said a boy named Sam.

He bounced a ball on his head. *Boing!*

And on his knees. *Boing!*

And on his nose. *Boing, boing!*

But Lollipop did not smile.

Amanda tried to think of a trick
she could do.
She wasn't very good at somersaults
or ball or hanging by her knees.
But she could dance.

"Look, Lollipop!" she said.
Amanda danced around the sandbox.
She twirled around the swings.

"And now for my pirouette," she said.

She spun around.

Faster and faster she went.

It was the most wonderful pirouette

she had ever done.

"Uh-oh," said Amanda.

Suddenly she felt dizzy.

The swings and slides and sandbox
all seemed to be spinning.
So were Lily and Sam and Sam's ball.

"Help!" cried Amanda.
The ball bounced on her head
and she fell into the sandbox.

Amanda opened her eyes.

There was Lollipop looking at her.

And she was smiling.

"She did it!" cried Amanda, jumping up.

"Lollipop smiled!"

And Lollipop smiled again.

PICTURES

"Our room is just perfect,"

said Mrs. Flora Pig.

"Except for one thing."

Amanda looked around.

"The walls are so plain," she said.

"They look lonely," said Lily.

"Exactly," said Mrs. Flora Pig.

"If only I had some nice pictures.

Pictures of you."

"We could make you some," said Amanda.

"Really big ones," said William.

"Good idea," said Mrs. Flora Pig.

She took out a long roll of paper.

"Lie down, please," she said.

She traced all around William.

Then she cut out a William shape.

"Now I have a life-size William

for my wall," she said.

"Do me!" said Amanda.

"And me!" said Sam.

Mrs. Flora Pig did everyone.
Then she put out scissors and glue
and crayons and buttons and beads
and bits of ribbon and lace
and all sorts of things.

"Now you can decorate
your pictures of you," she said.

Amanda worked hard on her picture.
First she colored her dress.
She used up a whole purple crayon.
Then she saw the lace. “Oh!” she said.
“I can make a ballet costume.”
She glued lace all over everything
and made ribbons for her hair.

Finally she drew the biggest smile
in all the world.

“I’m finished,” she said.

“How nice to have a happy Amanda for my wall,” said Mrs. Flora Pig. She hung Amanda on the wall next to William.

Soon everyone was on the wall. Everyone except Lollipop.

“Wow!” said Amanda. “Lollipop is coloring a hundred flowers.”

“Look,” said Sam.

“She even made a lollipop out of a button and a Popsicle stick.”

Lollipop smiled.

She colored her last flower.

"What a beautiful dress,"
said Mrs. Flora Pig.
She hung Lollipop on the wall
next to Amanda.

"Now my wall isn't lonely anymore,"
she said. "I have Lily and Sam
and William and Amanda and . . ."

Suddenly Lollipop was whispering

in Amanda's ear.

"Emily!" said Amanda.

"She told me her name. It's Emily."

Mrs. Flora Pig smiled.

"Welcome, Emily," she said.

They all cleaned up.

Then it was time to go home.

"Come on, Lollipop,
I mean Emily," said Amanda.
"We can sit together on the bus."
Emily whispered in her ear again.

"Okay," said Amanda.
"I will call you Lollipop."

Amanda took Lollipop's hand.

And together the two schoolgirls
walked through the wide halls
and up the high steps onto the bus.